THEY'RE FAMOUSE . . .
THEY'RE FABUMOUSE . . .
AND THEY'RE HERE
TO SAVE THE DAY!
THEY'RE THE

HEROM

AND THESE ARE THEIR
ADVENTURES!

Geronimo Stilton

CHARGE OF
THE CLONES

Scholastic Inc.

www.geronimostilton.com

Published by Scholastic Inc., *Publishers since 1920*, 557 Broadway, New York, NY 10012. SCHOLASTIC and associated logos are trademarks and/or registered trademarks of Scholastic Inc.

Stilton is the name of a famous English cheese. It is a registered trademark of the Stilton Cheese Makers' Association. For more information, go to www.stiltoncheese.com.

This book is a work of fiction. Names, characters, places, and incidents are either the product of the author's imagination or are used fictitiously, and any resemblance to actual persons, living or dead, business establishments, events, or locales is entirely coincidental.

ISBN 978-9-352-75155-6

Text by Geronimo Stilton
Original title *Superallarme, supertopo in fuga!*
Original design of the Heromice world by Giuseppe Facciotto and Flavio Ferron
Cover by Giuseppe Facciotto (design) and Daniele Verzini (color)
Illustrations by Luca Usai (pencils), Valeria Cairoli (inks), and Serena Gianoli and Daniele Verzini (color)
Graphics by Francesca Sirianni and Chiara Cebraro

Special thanks to Kathryn Cristaldi
Translated by Julia Heim
Interior design by Kevin Callahan / BNGO Books
First printing 2018

Reprinted by Scholastic India Pvt. Ltd., Feb. 2018

Printed in India by Repro India Ltd.

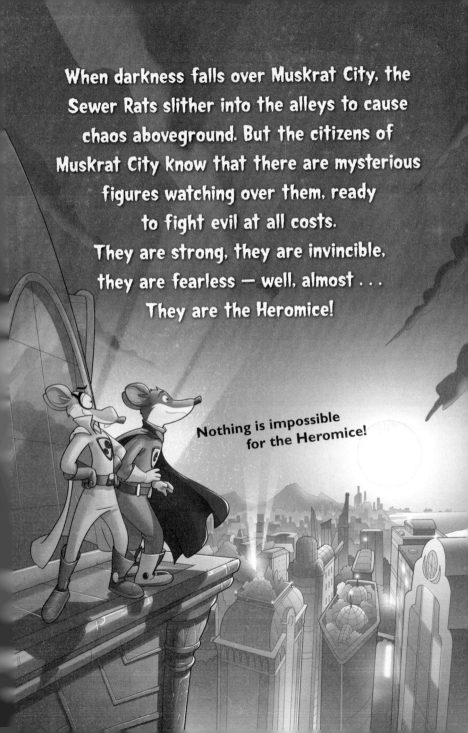

When darkness falls over Muskrat City, the Sewer Rats slither into the alleys to cause chaos aboveground. But the citizens of Muskrat City know that there are mysterious figures watching over them, ready to fight evil at all costs. They are strong, they are invincible, they are fearless — well, almost . . . They are the Heromice!

Nothing is impossible for the Heromice!

MEET THE HEROMICE!

GERONIMO SUPERSTILTON

The strongest hero in Muskrat City . . . but he still must learn how to control his powers!

SWIFTPAWS

Geronimo Superstilton's partner in crimefighting; he can transform his supersuit into anything.

LADY WONDERWHISKERS

A mysterious mouse with special powers; she always seems to be in the right place at the right time.

TESS TECHNOPAWS

A cook and scientist who assists the Heromice with every mission.

ELECTRON AND PROTON

Supersmart mouselets who help the Heromice; they create and operate sophisticated technological gadgets.

TONY SLUDGE

The undisputed leader of the Sewer Rats; known for being tough and mean.

SLICKFUR

Sludge's right-hand mouse; the true (and only) brains behind the Sewer Rats.

TERESA SLUDGE

Tony's wife; makes the important decisions for their family.

ELENA SLUDGE

Tony and Teresa's teenage daughter; has a real weakness for rat metal music.

ONE, TWO, AND THREE

Bodyguards who act as Sludge's henchmice; they are big, buff, and brainless.

I'M AN EXPERT!

It was a beautiful spring **morning**. The sun was shining, the birds were **SiNGiNG**, and the flowers were **BLOOMiNG**. It was a perfect day outside, but I was sitting in my office. The night before, two messengers had delivered the **TURBOCOPIER 9000**, our new high-tech photocopier. It was sleek, sophisticated, and **SUPeRCoMPLiCateD**!

I was reading the instructions manual when . . .

Oops! I'm sorry—I haven't introduced myself yet. My name is Stilton, *Geronimo Stilton*, and I am the *publisher* of *The Rodent's Gazette*, the most famous **newspaper** on Mouse Island!

Anyway, as I said, I was reading away when my cousin Trap **BURST** in.

"Trap!" I exclaimed. "What are you doing here?"

"Oh, not much, Germeister," he squeaked. "I just stopped in to say hi!"

Then he noticed the new superphotocopier. "Wow! Is

Hey, Cousin!

Huh?

that the Turbocopier 9000?" he asked. "I've always wanted to get my paws on one of those."

"Well, I haven't quite figured out how it works," I said.

"Ah, don't worry about reading the instructions, Cuz!" Trap replied, waving his paw dismissively. "I'm an **expert** on all things **electronic**!"

Before I could protest, he began HITTING buttons on the copier.

Nothing happened.

Then Trap's eyes lit up. "This might do the trick!" he exclaimed. With a loud smack, he hit a giant **RED** button on the side of the copier.

SSSQUIRttt!

A stream of ink shot out of the copier, staining my favorite green jacket.

Holey cheese, what a huge **DISASTER**!

"Oops, sorry, Ger." Trap giggled. "Hee, hee, hee! I was sure that was going to be the right button!"

Aaaack!

I was about to yell at him when the phone rang.

Riiiing! Riiiing! Riiiing!

Now what?

I picked up the phone.

"What took you so long, Geronimo?!" A familiar voice squeaked. It was my friend **HERCULE POIRAT**. He is also known as Swiftpaws, my Heromouse partner!

"Get your tail in gear, Geronimo! The Heromice are needed in Muskrat City! I'll be waiting for you at the Central Bank! Now **hurry**, **hurry**, **hurry**!"

"Um, what? I mean, how? I mean, why?" I babbled.

But it was too late. My hero partner had already hung up on me!

How rude!

Meanwhile, Trap was still PUNCHING buttons on the Turbocopier.

"Ahem, Trap, I need to run out," I squeaked as I headed for the door.

"No worries, Geronimo!" my cousin cried. "I'll handle the Turbocopier 9000. When you get back, it will work perfectly!"

I doubted it, but I couldn't worry about Trap or the copier. I had **BIGGER** problems!

Once I was outside, I ducked behind a lamppost and pressed the secret button on my Superpen.

Swoooooshhhh!

In an instant, I had transformed into my alter ego, Superstilton. The green superray surrounded me from my whiskers to my tail. Soon, I was flying through the air with my supercape BILLOWING behind me.

Too bad there was a hot air balloon festival taking place that day.

I bumped into one hot air balloon with my snout. *Bonk!*

Then I bounced into another balloon and landed on my tail. **Boing!**

Next, I crashed into a third balloon. **SMACK!**

Finally, I slammed into a fourth. **CRASH!**

Holey cheese balls, what a superblooper!

Help!

PAWS UP, SLUDGE!

Before long, I arrived at the Central Bank of Muskrat City. *Swiftpaws*, *Tess Technopaws* (the genius scientist and cook for the Heromice), and helpers **ELECTRON** and Proton were waiting for me.

Commissioner Rex Ratford was also there, yelling into a bullhorn, "Come out with your paws up, Tony Sludge!"

Immediately, my paws began shaking. Tony Sludge was the

Paws up, Sludge!

leader of a crew of **criminal** Sewer Rats. Whenever Tony appeared, trouble followed.

"Tony is in the b-b-bank?" I stuttered.

"Yep," Swiftpaws confirmed. "He's in there! The Sewer Rats were **robbing** the bank when the bank manager hit the **alarm**."

"Catching those cheeseheads will be a snap for us Heromice!" a voice added.

I **whirled** around and came snout-to-snout with the smart, **STRONG**, and beautiful Lady Wonderwhiskers! My heart began to **POUND WILDLY**. Oh, what a fascinating hero-rodent!

I was staring **dreamily** at my crush when Swiftpaws exclaimed, "HEROMICE IN ACTION!"

Then my hero colleagues raced into the bank, DRAGGING me along with them!

Inside the bank, the manager and the tellers were in a corner, gagged and tied up.

The safe was open, and the Sewer Rats were loading up **bags** of money!

Tony Sludge; his assistant, SLICKFUR; and his bodyguards, **ONE**, **TWO**, and **THREE**, didn't even notice us.

Heromice in action!

Let's go!

Swiftpaws snuck up behind them.

"Drop it, Sewer Slime!" he exclaimed.

The head of the Sewer Rats shot us an annoyed look. Then his henchmice, One, Two, and Three, came at us.

But with a series of super agile acrobatic jumps, Lady Wonderwhiskers fended off the rats and flipped to safety!

BONK! **POW!** **FLIP!**

Unfortunately, I was so distracted by my hero partner's *amazing* maneuvers that I didn't notice Two heading right for me! I turned suddenly, but it was too late!

"*Leaping liters of liquid Gorgonzola!*" I managed to squeak. "Get those paws off me!"

At those words, my superpowers activated.

Splaaaash!

Two was hit by a **WAVE** of

Huh?!

Ooooooh . . .

> **SUPERPOWER:**
> A WAVE OF MELTED GORGONZOLA ACTIVATED WITH THE CRY: "LEAPING LITERS OF LIQUID GORGONZOLA!"

Hee, hee, hee!

liquid Gorgonzola!

At the same time, Swiftpaws shouted,

"Costume: Super-Top Mode!"

In a flash, his costume transformed into a spinning yellow top that struck One and Three, sending them running in the opposite direction with their paws in the AIR.

Now that the three bodyguards were out of the picture, Tony and Slickfur looked around, confused.

"Give up, Sewer Rats!" Lady Wonderwhiskers ordered them.

"It's over, Sewer Slime!" Swiftpaws

chimed in. "This **heist** is history!"

Then something **incredible** happened. Tony Sludge and Slickfur **surrendered**!

Is It True?

Commissioner Ratford and the police strode into the bank. In the BLINK of an eye, Tony and the Sewer Rats were arrested, loaded into a van, and taken to the police station.

"Holey ham and Swiss!" Swiftpaws exclaimed. "That was as easy as drinking a super cream cheese smoothie!"

As we left the bank, we were greeted by loud shouts and cheers.

A huge crowd of excited rodents had gathered around the police barricade. There was even a television crew led by Blabberella, the famouse Muskrat TV anchormouse!

"And now, breaking news coming to you

live from the Central Bank of Muskrat City!" she squeaked, pointing the camera at Swiftpaws and me. "The **amazing** and superheroic Heromice have just captured the infamouse Sewer Rat gang!"

A group of photographers began snapping our pics as if we were celebrities on a RED CARPET! I turned as red as a tomato. Did I mention I'm a shy mouse at heart? Meanwhile, Swiftpaws struck a pose. Unlike me, my Heromouse partner LOVES being the center of attention!

"Is it true?" a voice squeaked from the crowd. It was Tess Technopaws. She pushed her way through the crowd to reach us. "Were the Sewer Rats really captured?!"

"They were!" Commissioner Ratford confirmed. "There's a cell waiting for them at MOUSECATRAZ PRISON!"

Electron and Proton joined us as well. "Superstilton, your mouserific cheesy powers were supercool!" said Proton.

"Superspectacular!" agreed Electron.

As everyone celebrated, I started thinking. With Tony in prison, my life would be completely transformed. **Good-bye**, phone calls from Swiftpaws at inconvenient times. **Good-bye**, flying at supersonic speeds to get to Muskrat City. **Good-bye**, hero friends.

Good-bye, Swiftpaws. **Good-bye** Lady Wonderwhiskers. **Good-bye**, Tess Technopaws, Electron, and Proton.

Sniff!

The more I thought about it, the sadder I became. I chewed my whiskers to stop myself from **bawling** like a newborn mouselet.

19

I glanced at Lady Wonderwhiskers and saw that she had a strange expression on her snout. Was she thinking what I was thinking? Was she going to miss being a Heromouse, too?

I was about to suggest we hold a yearly **Heromouse reunion** to keep in

Yay!

Sniff! Sniff!

Great work!

touch when Lady Wonderwhiskers let out a squeak first.

"Something's not right about this, Superstilton," she said. "Tony and Slickfur didn't even try to *flee*! It was much too easy to catch them!"

Commissioner Ratford was muttering into his cell phone. He looked serious. Suddenly, he yelped in shock. Then he ran toward us, a frightened look on his snout.

"You're not going to **believe** this, Heromice!" he cried. "But it seems as though there has been another burglary. This time it was at Muskrat Gems, the most famouse jewelry store in Muskrat City!"

Immediately, my whiskers began to *tremble* with fear.

Swiftpaws smiled SMUGLY.

"Don't worry, Commissioner," he said.

"Compared to capturing the Sewer Rats, stopping these thieves will be as easy as taking cheese from a **BLIND** rat!"

"But that's the problem," Ratford explained. "According to witnesses, the *Sewer Rats* were the thieves!"

ANOTHER GANG OF SEWER RATS?!

Swiftpaws's jaw nearly **HIT** the ground. "Tony Sludge is robbing a jewelry store?" he cried. "But that's impossible. He was just captured!"

The commissioner was as baffled as the rest of us. No one squeaked.

Lady Wonderwhiskers broke the silence. "We have to get to **Muskrat Gems** immediately!" she exclaimed.

Swiftpaws **SPRANG** into action. "Costume: Flying Scooter Mode!" he ordered.

ZAAAPPP!

Instantly, Swiftpaws had transformed himself into a **flying** scooter. Lady Wonderwhiskers jumped on. "**Come on, Superstilton!**" she urged.

I gulped. "Well, I, um . . ." I stalled. Did I mention I'm afraid of **heights**?"

"Stop **babbling**, hero partner!" Swiftpaws commanded. "Jump on!"

Oh, how do I get myself into these superscary situations?! Of course, I had no choice. I closed my eyes and jumped.

In a FLASH, we arrived at Muskrat Gems. The window was broken and the **alarm** was shrieking. We could see suspicious figures scampering around inside.

"Come out, Fontina Faces!" Lady Wonderwhiskers shouted.

At that moment, Tony, Slickfur, One, Two, and Three appeared before us.

"Galactic Gouda! I don't believe my eyes!" yelled Swiftpaws.

I couldn't believe mine, either! The Sewer Rats had just been taken to prison. But now

they were standing right in front of us!

Without missing a beat, the amazing Lady Wonderwhiskers charged ahead. Ah, what a **COURAGEOUS** super-rodent!

One, Two, and Three blocked her path as Tony and Slickfur dropped the jewels and ran.

Swiftpaws raced forward. "Hold it, **Sewer Slimeballs**!" he yelled.

B-but . . .

Heromice in action!

I was **FROZEN** with fear.

All of a sudden, I realized Two was about to hit Lady Wonderwhiskers! "**Whirling web of string cheese!**" I squeaked. "Watch out, hero partner!"

At those words, my superpowers activated.

Two webs of **SUPER-ELASTIC** string cheese fell over the Sewer Rats, trapping them!

"Great work, Superstilton!" cheered Lady Wonderwhiskers.

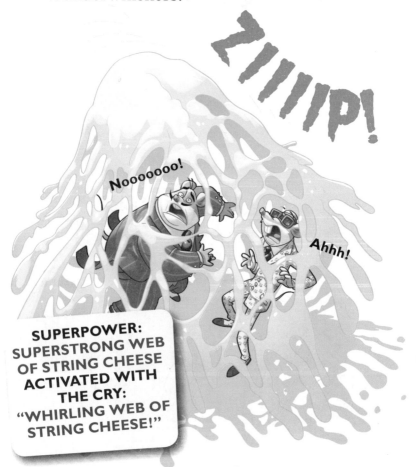

ZIIIIIP!

Nooooooo!

Ahhh!

SUPERPOWER: SUPERSTRONG WEB OF STRING CHEESE ACTIVATED WITH THE CRY: "WHIRLING WEB OF STRING CHEESE!"

Right at that moment, we heard police sirens approaching. At first I was relieved to see the commissioner. But when he jumped out of the car, I could tell something was wrong. His fur was as WHITE as a ball of mozzarella!

"Heromice, you'll never believe this," he squeaked. "An art gallery in Muskrat Plaza filled with priceless works has just been raided! And witnesses say the thieves are Tony and his gang!"

My eyes POPPED out of my fur. Well, okay, my eyes didn't really pop out, but you get the picture. Once again, I was shocked!

How could the Sewer Rats be in several places at once?

Then Commissioner Ratford told us some even more disturbing news. It seemed that the Sewer Rats had also been seen lurking

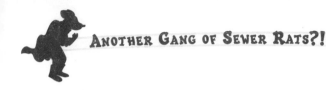

around **Precious Cheeses**, Muskrat City's premier cheese shop!

Good gravity! This case was getting **stranger** by the minute!

Bzzzz!

"*Supersonic Swiss slices!*" Swiftpaws exclaimed. "It sounds like Tony and his henchmice have a bunch of clones running around the city. We've got to stop them. I just wish I knew—"

BZZZZ!

My hero partner was interrupted midsentence by a **loud** sound. The sound seemed to be coming from the appliance store next to Muskrat Gems.

In the window, a display of different-sized television monitors was broadcasting a loud static humming sound along with a **fuzzy** image.

As we stood staring at the screens, the clear face of Tony Sludge appeared.

"Whoa! Way too much Tony!" Swiftpaws commented, holding up a paw.

"Good day, citizens of Muskrat City!"

Tony sneered. "I interrupt your regularly scheduled programming to give you this special announcement from your favorite rodent—me!" Tony cackled wildly.

"HA! HA! HA! HEE! HEE! HEE!"

The image on the screen changed.

Now it showed a large piece of equipment with a lot of buttons and flashing lights. Sludge's right-hand mouse, Slickfur, tinkered with the device, pulling levers and PUSHING buttons.

"And now I am happy to introduce to

you Slickfur's supergenius invention: the
RATOCOPIER!" Tony announced.

Slickfur pressed a red button, and the
machine began to run.

(1) First, a really powerful ray lit up
Tony . . .

(2) Then two flashes **SPARKED**,
surrounding him from the tip of his whiskers
to the end of his tail . . .

(3) Finally, a large tube spit out not just
ONE but **two** more Tonys! It deposited
them on a conveyer belt right before our
eyes!

"Thanks to the Ratocopier," the original
Tony explained, "we can now create
identical Sewer Rats!"

I gulped and glanced at Lady
Wonderwhiskers and Swiftpaws. They
looked very **WORRIED**. Now we knew

how **MULTIPLE** Sewer Rats were wreaking havoc on Muskrat City! We had to **stop** them!

Tony's sinister smile **SPREAD** from whisker to whisker. "Soon, thousands of my Ratocopies will invade Muskrat City! So, citizens, it's time to throw in the *cheesecloth*. You heard it here

Here we come . . .

Plop!

Plop!

first—Tony Sludge is taking over the city, and **no one** can stop me!"

And then Tony's snout disappeared.

"*Blistering blue cheese!*" Swiftpaws yelled at the **blank** screen, shaking his paw defiantly. "I will stop you!"

"And so will I!" Lady Wonderwhiskers chimed in.

I chewed my whiskers. Taking on one pack of Sewer Rats was hard enough. How were we going to handle *multiple* gangs? Still, I didn't want to seem like I wasn't a *team player*.

"Um, well, I guess, maybe I might be able to help, too . . ." I muttered under my breath.

"That's the **spirit**, Superstilton!" Swiftpaws cheered. "We will find Tony and destroy the Ratocopier! Isn't that right, hero partner?"

Bzzzz!

Ten plus thirty . . .

Whoa . . .

. . . a total mouserific disaster!

I glanced down the street. There were at least **ten** Ratocopied Tonys headed our way! And they were followed by about **thirty** Ratocopies of One, Two, and Three!

It all added up to a total mouserific **disaster**!

The Ratocopies advanced **threateningly**

as my whiskers **tRemBLeD** with fear. I wanted to turn tail and run, but not my hero partner. Swiftpaws nodded at Lady Wonderwhiskers and then at me.

"We can do this!" he squeaked. Then he shouted our battle cry:

"HEROMICE IN ACTION!"

MULTIPLYING MONSTER RATS!

The **Ratocopies** continued their march toward us. Together, they looked like one **massive**, **MENACING** mouse army. In fact, there were so many of them, they took up the whole street!

Multiplying monster rats! How could three Heromice take on an entire army? We needed an idea . . . and fast!

Suddenly, Swiftpaws yelled, **"Costume: Rubber Band Mode!"**

Within seconds, he had transformed into a super rubber band that **stretched** across the street.

As soon as the first line of Sewer Rats

reached the band, they **tripped**, **ROLLED**, and fell flat on their snouts! The second row fell on top of the first. And the third fell on top of the second! Pretty soon, the whole army lay in an enormouse heap on the ground!

Ratford and his mice arrested them at once.

While the Ratocopies were being taken to

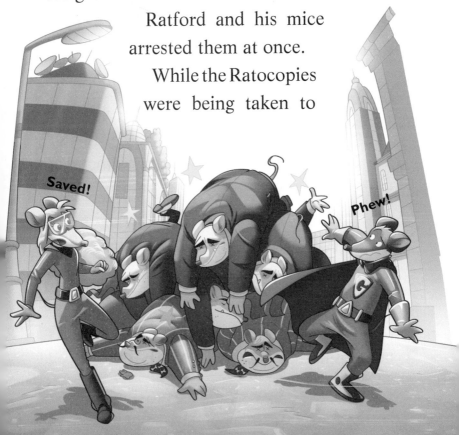

Saved!

Phew!

the police station, Swiftpaws puffed up his fur. "I told you, dear Heromouse partners, nothing is impossible for the **HEROMICE**!" he boasted.

I have to admit, I was feeling super good about everything when disaster struck. A second group of Ratocopies **POPPED** up from around the corner!

"Good gravity! Let's get out of here!" Swiftpaws yelled as he ducked into an alley.

We followed him, paws flying as quickly as possible. But the Tony Sludge Ratocopies were right behind us!

Swiftpaws turned **RIGHT**, then *left*, then **RIGHT** again. *Where, oh, where was he going?*

"I don't know if I can make it!" I wailed, *huffing* and puffing. I knew I shouldn't have quit that **scamperobics** class I had signed up for at the gym. My paws were aching and my heart was **POUNDING** out of my fur!

Still, Swiftpaws kept going. "Come on, hero partners! Follow me!" he shrieked, racing off.

But after a few more turns, Swiftpaws slowed down. "I thought we were close, but . . ." he muttered.

Just then we turned the corner and found ourselves at a **dead end**. At the far end of the street was a **PHONE BOOTH**. How strange.

"Quick, everyone inside!" Swiftpaws squeaked, slipping into the booth.

Which way?

"All **three** of us won't fit!" I cried.
But my superpartners yanked me in behind them.

When all three of us were in the **booth**, Swiftpaws began to press a **SUPERLONG** sequence of numbers into the phone.

5 . . . 6 . . . 1 . . . 6 . . .

7 . . . 3 . . . 2 . . . I gulped. The Ratocopies were almost at the booth!

Still, my hero partner calmly continued to punch in numbers.

Who was he calling?! "Um, Swiftpaws, this probably isn't a great time to make a phone call," I commented.

"**SHHHH!**" he replied,

Hooray!

Here it is!

A phone booth?

annoyed. "Don't make me lose count!"

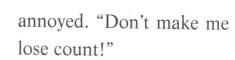

7 . . . 4 . . . 3 . . . 5 . . .

BLAM!

The strangest thing happened. The floor of the booth opened and we **slid** down a steep **UNDERGROUND** tunnel!

"You see?" Swiftpaws said, chuckling.

"But where

Wahoo!

Hee, hee!

Help!

are we **gooooiiiinnngg**?" I yelled, terrified.

We continued to fall down, down, down at rattastic speeds until . . . **bonk**!

We landed in a small, **windowless** room.

I looked around in a panic. Was it my imagination, or were the walls **CLOSING** in on us? Have I mentioned that I'm afraid of **TIGHT** spaces?

Lady Wonderwhiskers was the first to stand up. "Where are we?" she asked.

Swiftpaws grinned. "Don't worry, hero partners! It's all under control! Let me explain . . ."

It turns out the phone booth led to a secret passage. It had been built by Swiftpaws's grandfather **Pierre Poirat**, the first **supercourageous** Heromouse of Muskrat City!

"By dialing the **SECRET CODE**, we gained access to this room," Swiftpaws explained. "We're just steps away from the basement of **Heromice Headquarters**!"

"Well, what are we waiting for?" Lady Wonderwhiskers replied, grinning. "Let's go!"

SUPER INFRAMOUSE RAY GLOVE!

We left the secret room using a door hidden in a wall. The door led to a long, NARROW corridor, which led to Heromice Headquarters!

Electron and Proton came to greet us. "WELCOME, HEROMICE!" they squeaked excitedly.

As we entered the control room, Tess Technopaws rushed over. "Great gobs of Gouda!" she exclaimed. "It's good to see you. Come look at this!"

The screens of the supercomputer were transmitting the news. Melted mozzarella! The images passing

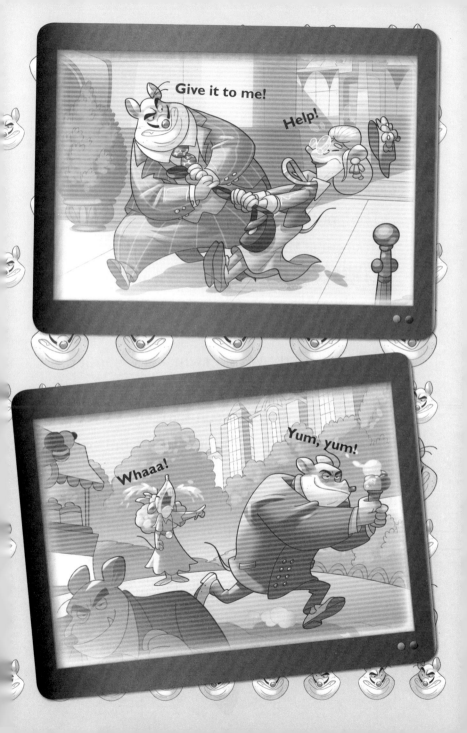

before our eyes confirmed our worst fears. Muskrat City had fallen into complete **chaos**!

The police were trying to block the Ratocopies, but they were everywhere!

"**Twisted cat tails!**" I wailed. "We'll never be able to stop all of them!"

"Unless we manage to find their weakest point . . . " Lady Wonderwhiskers wondered aloud, her voice **trailing** off.

Electron smiled mischievously. "Well, I think we may have found out an important **SECRET** about the Ratocopies that just may prove useful," he squeaked.

"What is it?" Swiftpaws demanded.

"We did some studies of the Ratocopies that were captured at the bank," Electron explained.

"The Ratocopier is a **3-D** printer.

It's making three-dimensional copies of the Sewer Rats. But they're just copies. They obey Tony's orders, but they can't think for themselves."

"And it appears that the Ratocopies are sensitive to the light of the **inframouse ray**," Tess Technopaws chimed in.

She held up a strange-looking glove. It was her latest invention, the Super Inframouse Ray Glove. "One flash from this glove and the Ratocopies should *disappear*! I haven't been able to test it out yet. That will be your job, Heromice!"

Blistering blue cheese!

"Um, w-well, b-but . . ." I stammered, protesting.

But my hero partner was already on his way out the door with one of Tess's prototypes.

"We'll do it!" he cried. "Now let's get to the police station. There's no time to waste!"

When we arrived, the commissioner was trying FRANTICALLY to respond to all the **emergency** calls from citizens.

"The jail cells are already PACKED with Ratocopies!" Ratford lamented.

What can we do, Heromice?

Umm . . .

"It's okay, Commissioner!" Swiftpaws said. "We've got a **plan**!"

My hero partner held up Tess's invention.

"This glove can defeat a Ratocopy faster than you can say 'super Swiss slices'!" he gloated.

Swiftpaws approached a **cell** with two Tony Ratocopies locked inside.

"Let's try taking a PICTURE of this

We've got a plan!

no-good Sewer Rat!" he said.

Then he pointed Tess's glove at the Ratocopy.

Flash!

Ahhh!

Within seconds . . . poof! The Ratocopy had DEMATERIALIZED before our eyes!

SWIRLING TORNADO OF SWISS ROLLS!

"Super Swiss rolls!" Swiftpaws rejoiced. "This thing really works!"

Then he pointed the glove at another jail cell full of Ratocopies.

Flash! **Flash!** **Flash!**

After a few minutes, there wasn't a single Ratocopy left at the police station.

"**FABUMOUSE!**" Ratford exclaimed.

At that moment, my wrist communicator began to beep.

It was a call from **HEROMICE HEADQUARTERS**.

Lady Wonderwhiskers appeared on the screen. "Base to Superstilton, is everything okay?" she asked. "Did you try Tess's iNVENTiON?"

"We sure did, Lady Wonderwhiskers!" Swiftpaws said. "It worked like a charm!"

The hero-rodent of my dreams beamed. Then she asked us to meet her at **City Hall**. "I have a plan to get **RID** of all the Ratocopies at once!"

"B-but how will we g-get there?" I stammered. "The streets are full of R-r-r-ratocopies!"

"Nothing is impossible for the Heromice!" she replied, winking at me.

Then the image disappeared.

I cringed. How many times did I have to say it? **I'm not cut out to be a Heromouse!**

Still, I couldn't let Lady Wonderwhiskers down. Too bad the FASTEST way to City Hall was flying. Oh, how I hate to fly! Luckily, my Heromouse partner had a solution.

He transformed himself into a supercatapult and . . .

Swoosh!

He launched me toward the roof of City Hall!

From above, we could see all the streets that had been invaded by Ratocopies. Good gravity!

Gulp!

Get ready, Superstilton!

There were tons of Slickfurs and Tonys!

Then we saw the athletic and courageous Lady Wonderwhiskers. She wasn't ALONE, and she had one of Tess's prototypes, too. Proton and Electron were with her in front of City Hall.

As we watched, a group of Ratocopies of ONE, TWO, and Three set out to capture them. The Ratocopies surrounded our friends, but Lady Wonderwhiskers pointed the **Super Inframouse Ray Glove** at them and . . .

Flash! **Flash!** **Flash!**

The Ratocopies dematerialized, leaving behind a bunch of colorful sparkles.

But seconds later, at least thirty

Ugh!

Stay back!

Ratocopies of Tony entered the square.

"Superstilton! Swiftpaws! Help!" shrieked Electron and Proton.

Swiftpaws flew toward our friends. "HEROMOUSE NOSEDIVE!" he yelled.

He grabbed the two **mouselets**, pulling them to safety.

I followed my hero colleague's example and darted downward.

WHOOOSH!

I flew toward Lady Wonderwhiskers like a real Heromouse. "Hold on, Lady Wonderwhiskers!" I exclaimed, grabbing the hero-rodent's paws. But just before I could take off, a Tony Ratocopy managed to grab on to Lady Wonderwhisker's **boot**!

"Help!" she shouted.

"Swirling tornado of Swiss rolls!" I squeaked. "Let go of her!"

At those words, a **TORNADO** of Swiss rolls hit the Ratocopy. He immediately let go of Lady Wonderwhiskers and landed with a splash in the fountain in the middle of the square.

SPLAAAASH!

"*Nice work, Superstilton!*" cheered Swiftpaws as we landed on the roof of City Hall.

SUPERPOWER: A TORNADO OF SWISS ROLLS ACTIVATED WITH THE CRY: "SWIRLING TORNADO OF SWISS ROLLS!"

Wow!

Hang on!

Oof!

THE SUPERMEGAFLASH

Lady Wonderwhiskers's lovely blue eyes **SHONE** with admiration.

"You saved me, Superstilton!" she squeaked. "I would have never escaped without your help!"

Thank you!

It was nothing!

Instantly, I turned as RED as a supertomato. "Oh, it was nothing, Lady Whiskers, I mean, **Lady Wonderful**, uh, I mean, Lady Wonderwhiskers," I babbled nervously.

Ugh. How embarrassing. Just once, I wish I wouldn't turn into a stammering fool in front of my favorite Heromouse.

I was trying to think of something clever to say when Proton and Electron arrived.

"We brought the Supermegaflash, another one of Tess's fabumouse inventions. It can transform electric light into inframouse rays!" Proton said. He showed us a contraption full of levers, lights, and buttons.

"Now all we have to do is hook it up to Muskrat City's electricity," Electron explained. "Then every streetlight in the city will become a super potent ray capable of DESTROYING the Ratocopies!"

"Perfect!" Lady Wonderwhiskers said, putting her arms around the two mouselets.

We decided that Lady Wonderwhiskers would go with Electron and Proton to set up the Supermegaflash. "We'll attach it to the **electricity transmitter tower** at the top of the great hill that overlooks Muskrat City," Electron said.

"That's a fantastic idea," agreed Lady Wonderwhiskers. Then she turned to Swiftpaws.

"While we're busy setting up the **SUPERMEGAFLASH**," she said, "you and Superstilton can get to work on the second part of the plan. It will be superdangerous and superscary, but you two can handle it."

Superdangerous? Superscary? Immediately, my heart began to **pound** so hard I thought it might **POP** right out of my fur! Well, okay, I didn't *really* think it would **POP** out, but you get it. I was scared silly!

"Of course!" Swiftpaws agreed. "Nothing is too difficult for us Heromice! So what's the plan?"

"You two will need to locate and destroy the Ratocopier!" said Lady Wonderwhiskers.

I blinked. "B-b-but how will we find it?" I stammered.

"We have some idea, Heromice!" Electron exclaimed. "Do you remember Tony's message on TV this morning? The one where he was showing off Slickfur's new invention? Well, we managed to locate the origin of the TV SIGNAL. The Sewer Rats transmit from somewhere on the outskirts of Muskrat City!"

Swiftpaws winked at me. "Super Swiss slices! That'll save us a nice trip to the sewers!"

I nodded. I was thrilled we didn't have to brave the stinky sewers. Still, I wasn't looking forward to *prowling* around the outskirts of Muskrat City, either. Who knew what other dangers lurked there?

I was trying not to think about the scary possibilities when my **Heromouse watch** activated. Tess's smiling face appeared on the screen. "Good news, Heromice! I have an idea of where the Sewer Rats may have hidden the Ratocopier. There are some abandoned *warehouses* on the outskirts of Muskrat City that are big enough to hide the contraption!"

"**LET'S GO!**" cried Swiftpaws.

Don't get me wrong. I was terrified. But with the moon **GLOWING** and my cape flapping in the wind, I also felt superspecial.

What an adventure!

Bonk! Pow! Bop!

While Swiftpaws and I took off in search of the abandoned warehouses, Lady Wonderwhiskers and the mouselets made their way toward the **transmitter tower**.

Suddenly, a Ratocopy POPPeD out of an oversized trash bin. "Look out!" yelled Electron.

Lady Wonderwhiskers pointed the glove at the Ratocopy and . . .

Flash!

Flash!

Flash!

The Ratocopy vanished in a cloud of **golden sparkles**.

"Yes!" Proton exclaimed.

Dusk was falling as Lady Wonderwhiskers, Electron, and Proton continued their hunt for Ratocopies. Before long, it was **COMPLETELY DARK**. Suddenly, Proton felt someone grab him from behind.

"**Help!**" he screamed. "**THEY GOT ME!**"

Lady Wonderwhiskers turned on her **flashlight** and pointed it at Proton.

Hey!

Everything okay, Proton?

Electron **burst** out laughing. "Ha, ha!" she giggled. "A branch just got caught on your backpack! You're not scared, are you, Proton?"

Proton tried to laugh, too, but a minute

Help!

later his eyes **widened** in alarm.

"What is it now?" Electron asked, still chuckling. Then she looked up and turned as *pale* as a slice of provolone.

Nine **Ratocopies** of Tony had just popped out from behind some bushes.

Lady Wonderwhiskers turned on the SUPER INFRAMOUSE RAY GLOVE and made the first of the Ratocopies disappear.

Flash! **Flash!** **Flash!**

"Yes!" Proton cheered, PUMPING his paw in the air.

Lady Wonderwhiskers **zapped** more Ratocopies.

Flash! **Flash!** **Flash!**

But then . . .

Bzzzzooottt!

"What happened, Lady Wonderwhiskers?" asked Electron.

"Hmm . . . it looks like the **glove** needs to be recharged," the Heromouse said calmly.

"W-w-what do we d-d-do n-n-now?" stammered Proton.

There were still four Ratocopies left in the clearing.

"I'll just have to use more traditional methods with these pests!" Lady Wonderwhiskers replied confidently.

Then she took one **super-agile**, *superspeedy*, super-elegant jump . . . and knocked all the Ratocopies out in one go!

BONK! POW! BOP!

Lady Wonderwhiskers pulled a **rope** out of her belt and **wrapped** it around the Ratocopies, tying them up like the **perfect** cheese enchilada.

"Wow! That was *awesome*, Lady Wonderwhiskers!" Proton exclaimed with

Awesome, Lady Wonderwhiskers!

Yay!

Take that, pests!

admiration. "Maybe someday you could teach me how to **TIE** up criminals like that!"

Lady Wonderwhiskers grinned. "Sure! **Nothing to it!**" she declared.

Electron giggled. "First you'd have to teach him the difference between a **TREE BRANCH** and a criminal," she snorted.

Lady Wonderwhiskers put her arms around the two mouselets. "Come on," she squeaked. "We'd better get to the tower as quickly as we can. **Time's ticking!**"

Don't Look Down!

As Lady Wonderwhiskers and the mouselets climbed the hill to set up Tess's SUPERINVENTION, Swiftpaws and I landed in the outskirts of Muskrat City after a superclose flight between skyscrapers.

Aside from the houses, there was a stretch of abandoned factories, WAREHOUSES, and storage facilities, just as Tess had said. It didn't take long to find the Sewer Rats' hideout. There were dozens of Ratocopies of ONE, TWO, and Three keeping guard in the courtyard of one of the buildings!

Luckily, the RATOCOPIES weren't the sharpest cheese knives in the drawer. As soon as the Sewer Rat guarding the entrance was distracted, we entered the building.

Holey aged gorgonzola!

The warehouse was jam-packed with Ratocopies!

There were a hundred Tonys and an equal number of Slickfurs! In the middle of the warehouse, the Ratocopier **churned**

away. Every few minutes, another Ratocopy joined the others!

As we watched, the real **Sewer Rats** (not the Ratocopies) congratulated themselves.

"Tomorrow will be the final **showdown**!"

Tony snickered. "Then Muskrat City will be mine, mine, mine!"

How did we know who the *real* Sewer Rats were? By now, we had discovered a difference between the two. The Ratocopies never **BLINKED**!

"What a cosmic catastrophe!" Swiftpaws whispered. "We need to stop Slickfur's machine right away!"

"B-b-but how?" I stammered.

Swiftpaws had an idea. He pointed to a **rusty** ladder. It led to a walkway that **HUNG** directly over the Ratocopier.

"We'll **climb** over!" he announced.

My heart **pounded** under my fur. Did I mention I'm afraid of heights?

"Are you sure, hero partner?" I stammered, **twisting** my tail. "That ladder looks rusty—"

"Are you or aren't you a
HEROMOUSE?"
Swiftpaws interrupted me.

I tried to explain that I
am not cut out to be a
Heromouse, but as usual
my hero partner didn't
seem to hear me.

Instead, he dragged
me over to the
ladder. What could
I do? I began to
CLIMB . . .

As I climbed, I gave
myself a pep talk. It
went like this:
**Don't look down!
Don't look down!
Don't look down!**

Gulp!

Keep going!

Far below us, we could hear One, Two, and Three talking to Slickfur.

"Um, Boss?" asked One. "Do you think we could get our **Ratocopies** now?"

"You **PROMISED** we could each have one," added Two.

"That's right," agreed Three.

"I'm going to call mine FOUR!" said One.

"I'm calling mine *Five*!" added Two.

"And I'm calling mine . . ." began Three.

But he never finished. Slickfur had flown into a rage. "Forget it, you fools!" he shrieked. "The Ratocopies aren't toys!"

Meanwhile, Swiftpaws and I had arrived on the walkway that hung in MIDAIR. Holey cheese! We were so HIGH up, my head began to feel light. Oh no! Was I going to faint? Suddenly, the whole walkway began

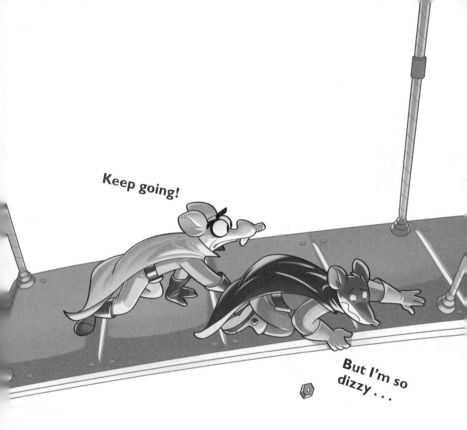

Keep going!

But I'm so dizzy . . .

to wobble and SHAKE!

I reached for the side to steady myself and accidentally knocked off a loose bolt. **Clonk!**

The bolt rolled toward the edge of the walkway and fell down . . . down . . . down . . . To my horror, it landed right on

Tony's head. It **BOUNCED** off his fur and *rolled* to the ground.

Boing! Boing! Boing!

"Hey! What was that?" he growled.

Then Tony, Slickfur, One, Two, and Three looked up and **SPOTTED** us.

"Intruders!" the head of the Sewer Rats tHUNDeReD.

Swiftpaws and I looked at each other in a panic. Getting discovered was not part of our plan! What a superdisaster!

STOP THAT MACHINE!

After a really strong initial case of the *supertrembles*, Swiftpaws took control of the situation. "That's it, Sewer Slimes! **STOP** that machine at once or you'll have to deal with the Heromice!" he squeaked.

"Ooooh, I'm so scared!" Tony snickered.

He ordered his henchmice to capture us. Dozens and dozens of **ONES**, **TWOS**, and **THREES** approached the ladder, trying to reach us.

"You're finished now, superpests!" the head of the Sewer Rats yelled, eyes *FLASHING* wickedly.

The Ratocopies began to climb up the

RUSTY ladder. The ladder groaned with every step. I closed my eyes. Blistering blue cheese! Is this how it would all end?

"I am *so* not cut out to be a Heromouse!" I sobbed.

But, just then, the most amazing thing happened. I heard a loud screeching sound, so I opened my eyes. GREAT BALLS OF MOZZARELLA! The *rusty* metal ladder had become detached from the wall. It crashed to the ground, taking the Ratocopies with it!

Ka-blam! Ka-blam!

"Ratocopies, get into **PYRAMID FORMATION**!" Tony thundered.

Uh-oh. That didn't sound good!

The Ratocopies climbed onto one another's backs, forming a super rat pyramid!

Get ready!

I was ready to give up when Swiftpaws shouted,

"Costume: Bouncing Ball Mode!"

He transformed himself into a gigantic rubber ball and bounced through the air.

BOING!
BOING!
BOING!

He crashed into the pyramid, toppling it!

But more Ratocopies quickly formed another pyramid!

Rotten cheddar rinds! It seemed like things couldn't get any worse.

Climb...

Climb...

Climb...

Climb...

Climb...

Climb...

Climb...

Climb...

Climb...

And then they did!

One of the chains LINKING the walkway to the roof suddenly snapped!

Craaaaack!

I lost my balance, slipped, and found myself dangling in midair!

"Help!" I squeaked at the top of my lungs. I was about to become one FLATTENED rodent!

"HOLEY HAILING CHEDDAR BITES!"

At those words, my Heromouse superpowers activated. A HAILSTORM of *cheddar bites* crashed down from above.

The Ratocopies ran for cover.

"Look out!" yelled the Ones.

"They're **ATTACKING**!" screeched the Twos.

"Mmmm . . . tasty!" commented the Threes.

While the Ratocopies were **pelted** with cheese bites, Slickfur and Tony hid in a corner of the room.

"Give it up, superfools!" Slickfur snorted. "Do you really think this cheesy little HAILSTORM is enough to stop us?"

"The Ratocopier is made of super-reinforced steel! Cheddar bites won't shut it down!" added Tony.

Right at that moment, I noticed a cheddar bite had **rolled** into the Ratocopier. A minute later, the machine began to hum.

First there was a strong RAY OF LIGHT that lit the cheese.

Then a short while later . . .

Splutt! Splutt! Splutt!

Thousands of cheddar cheese bites began to tumble out of the Ratocopier, filling up the entire warehouse and crushing the Ratocopies!

Sweet cherry chunk cheesecake! What a super sight!

As the Sewer Rats (the real ones) tried to **scramble** to safety, I let myself fall from the walkway. I landed on a nice, soft mountain of cheese bites.

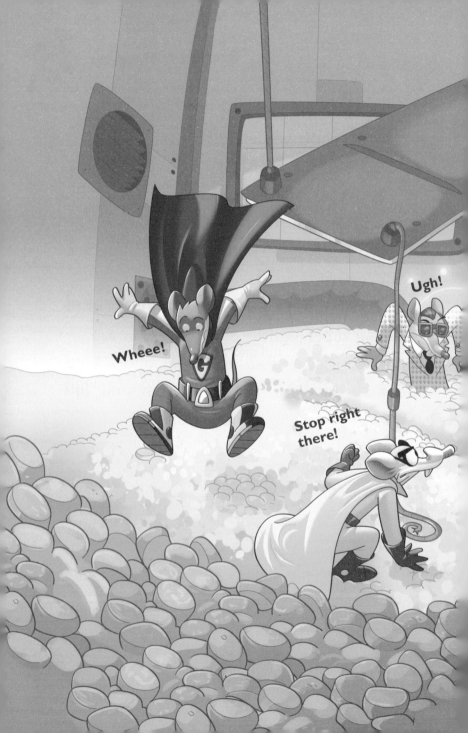

SUPER LIGHTS!

Swiftpaws high-fived me. "Great **GOBS** of Gruyère! Nice move, hero partner!"

"Er, thanks," I mumbled. I was glad my **superpowers** had stopped the Ratocopies. Still, it's hard to take credit for something you did when you're not really sure how you did it! Maybe one of these days I'd figure out exactly how my superpowers worked . . .

A **SHOUT** from Tony Sludge broke into my thoughts. He was standing on the top of a mound of cheese.

"You'll never get us!" he cried, hitting the button on a remote control.

Vrooooommm!

Immediately, the Sewer Rats' armored limousine, the Drillmobile, popped out of the cheese.

"So long, superfools!" Tony sneered as he climbed aboard. "You *destroyed* the Ratocopier but not the Ratocopies that have taken over the city!"

A moment later, the Drillmobile *disappeared* underground.

"Let's follow them!" Swiftpaws exclaimed, super determined.

I really wanted to take a CHEESE BREAK. (Those cheddar bites looked delicious!) But I knew what we had to do.

"Wait!" I told my Heromouse partner. "We need to deal with the other Ratocopies and save Muskrat City!"

So, in the end, we returned to the city, where we were approached by a group

of Ratocopies. Luckily, we managed to **FLASH** them with the *inframouse rays* from Tess's superglove.

FLASH! FLASH! FLASH! FLASH!
FLASH! FLASH! FLASH! FLASH!

Still, it wasn't long before more Ratocopies appeared. After a few minutes, we were surrounded once again!

RANCID RAT HAIRS!

While we were battling the Ratocopies, Lady Wonderwhiskers, Proton, and Electron were gathered on the other side of town. They had just arrived at the transmitter tower.

Proton carefully opened the *electrical box* and began hitting buttons.

"Do you remember the **numeric code** so we can activate the SUPERMEGAFLASH?" asked Electron.

Proton gave him the code, and a second later the connection was complete! All the streetlamps of Muskrat City lit up with a super bright, **BLINDING** light!

BZZZZZZZTTT!

A flash **LiT UP** the night and hit the Ratocopies, dematerializing them into millions of tiny *colorful* sparkles!

We've almost got it . . .

Great work!

Bzzzaaappp!

"Super Swiss slices!" Swiftpaws exclaimed. "What just happened?" We watched in amazement as the Ratocopies **disappeared** before our eyes.

I pointed to the lights coming from the transmitter tower. "Lady Wonderwhiskers and the mouselets have done it!" I squeaked happily. "They must have hooked up the **Supermegaflash** and activated the lights.

As I spoke, the FLASHING continued. One by one, the Ratocopies were ZAPPED into oblivion! In fact, by now, the entire city was lit up in that fabumouse anti–Sewer Rat light!

Mission Accomplished!

When we got back to the base, we were in for a **treat**. And I mean, a *real* treat! Tess greeted us with a tray of her *super-fried mozzarella balls*. They were **hot**, crispy, and whisker-licking delicious!

"Welcome back, Heromice!" she exclaimed, giving us each a **hug**.

Lady Wonderwhiskers, Proton, and Electron were gathered around the **television** watching the news.

"Thanks to the Heromice, the Ratocopies

have been dematerialized," the reporter announced with a grin. "And just look at that amazing **fireworks** display! Muskrat City is **SAFE** at last!"

I smiled. **Mission accomplished!** It was time to return to New Mouse City.

I said good-bye to my friends and prepared to fly back home.

"I'm sure those rotten Sewer Rats will be back again," Electron said, wrapping her paws around me. "But at least we know that the **HEROMICE** will always be here to protect us!"

Swiftpaws chuckled. "You got it!" he agreed. "Like I always say, nothing is impossible for us **Heromice**! Right, Superstilton?"

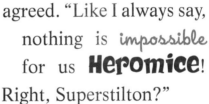

Aww!

Thanks!

"Um, er, well, yes, I guess . . ." I mumbled. What could I say? I'm afraid to fly, and I don't quite understand my own superpowers. Still, no one ever listened when I explained I'm not cut out to be a Heromouse. So I just smiled and **waved** good-bye.

Then, without any warning, my **supercostume** suddenly took off, taking me with it! I was racing through the sky at full speed toward NEW MOUSE CITY!

I landed not far from *The Rodent's Gazette*. A second later, my costume switched back to my usual green suit. Even though it was late, I decided to go to the office to check on things. When I opened the door, I heard a *buzzing* sound.

Bzzzzzzzzz!

How strange. What was that?

Then I remembered . . .

When I left for my hero **ADVENTURE**, Trap had been in charge of figuring out how to work the new photocopier! Now the TURBOCOPIER 9000 was up and running, and it was shooting out copies at *full speed*!

HOLEY CHEESE BALLS! The machine was out of control! It was spitting out copies as fast as Tony's terrifying Ratocopier!

Luckily, they were just paper photocopies and not dangerous copies of the Sewer Rats. In fact, the only SCARY thing about these copies was that they had my cousin's snout **plastered** all over them!

I looked around, but there was no sign of Trap anywhere.

I searched for the OFF SWITCH on the copier, but I couldn't find it. I decided I had only one choice—I PULLED the plug!

Finally, there was peace and quiet!

A minute later, I noticed a **BLUE** piece of paper taped to my desk lamp. It was from Trap.

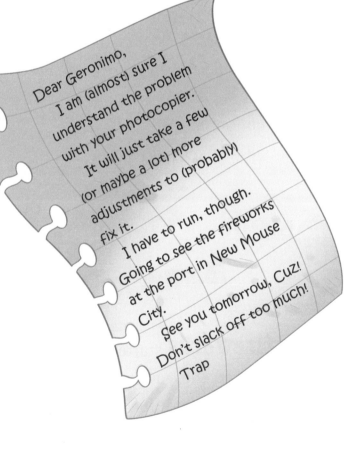

Dear Geronimo,
I am (almost) sure I understand the problem with your photocopier.
It will just take a few (or maybe a lot) more adjustments to (probably) fix it.
I have to run, though. Going to see the fireworks at the port in New Mouse City.
See you tomorrow, Cuz! Don't slack off too much!
Trap

I rolled my eyes. Why was I not surprised? I was used to cleaning up my cousin's big messes. I scooped up all the sheets with Trap's face on them. Then I sat down at my desk and pulled out a trusty piece of literature.

"Here we are!" I exclaimed. "The good old instruction manual!"

I had just started reading when . . .

the fireworks started.

I went to the window to enjoy the show. The sky was beautiful, lit up by COLORFUL sparkles.

As I watched the fireworks, I couldn't help but think of my adventure in Muskrat City. The colorful sparkles looked just like the sparkles from the Ratocopies when they were hit with the **Supermegaflash.**

See you later, Sewer Rats! I chuckled to myself.

NOTHING IS IMPOSSIBLE FOR THE HEROMICE!

Be sure to read all my fabumouse adventures!

#1 Lost Treasure of the Emerald Eye

#2 The Curse of the Cheese Pyramid

#3 Cat and Mouse in a Haunted House

#4 I'm Too Fond of My Fur!

#5 Four Mice Deep in the Jungle

#6 Paws Off, Cheddarface!

#7 Red Pizzas for a Blue Count

#8 Attack of the Bandit Cats

#9 A Fabumouse Vacation for Geronimo

#10 All Because of a Cup of Coffee

#11 It's Halloween, You 'Fraidy Mouse!

#12 Merry Christmas, Geronimo!

#13 The Phantom of the Subway

#14 The Temple of the Ruby of Fire

#15 The Mona Mousa Code

#16 A Cheese-Colored Camper

#17 Watch Your Whiskers, Stilton!

#18 Shipwreck on the Pirate Islands

#19 My Name Is Stilton, Geronimo Stilton

#20 Surf's Up, Geronimo!

#21 The Wild, Wild West

#22 The Secret of Cacklefur Castle

A Christmas Tale

#23 Valentine's Day
Disaster

#24 Field Trip to
Niagara Falls

#25 The Search for
Sunken Treasure

#26 The Mummy
with No Name

#27 The Christmas
Toy Factory

#28 Wedding
Crasher

#29 Down and Out
Down Under

#30 The Mouse Island
Marathon

#31 The Mysterious
Cheese Thief

Christmas Catastrophe

#32 Valley of the
Giant Skeletons

#33 Geronimo and the
Gold Medal Mystery

#34 Geronimo Stilton,
Secret Agent

#35 A Very Merry
Christmas

#36 Geronimo's
Valentine

#37 The Race Across
America

#38 A Fabumouse
School Adventure

#39 Singing Sensation

#40 The Karate Mouse

#41 Mighty Mount
Kilimanjaro

#42 The Peculiar
Pumpkin Thief

#43 I'm Not a
Supermouse!

#44 The Giant
Diamond Robbery

#45 Save the White
Whale!

#46 The Haunted
Castle

#47 Run for the Hills, Geronimo!

#48 The Mystery in Venice

#49 The Way of the Samurai

#50 This Hotel Is Haunted!

#51 The Enormouse Pearl Heist

#52 Mouse in Space!

#53 Rumble in the Jungle

#54 Get into Gear, Stilton!

#55 The Golden Statue Plot

#56 Flight of the Red Bandit

The Hunt for the Golden Book

#57 The Stinky Cheese Vacation

#58 The Super Chef Contest

#59 Welcome to Moldy Manor

The Hunt for the Curious Cheese

#60 The Treasure of Easter Island

#61 Mouse House Hunter

#62 Mouse Overboard!

The Hunt for the Secret Papyrus

#63 The Cheese Experiment

#64 Magical Mission

#65 Bollywood Burglary

The Hunt for the Hundredth Key

#66 Operation: Secret Recipe

Check out these very special editions!

**THEA STILTON:
THE JOURNEY
TO ATLANTIS**

**THEA STILTON:
THE SECRET OF
THE FAIRIES**

**THEA STILTON:
THE SECRET OF
THE SNOW**

**THEA STILTON:
THE CLOUD
CASTLE**

**THEA STILTON:
THE TREASURE
OF THE SEA**

**THE JOURNEY
THROUGH TIME**

**BACK IN TIME:
THE SECOND JOURNEY
THROUGH TIME**

**THE RACE
AGAINST TIME:
THE THIRD JOURNEY
THROUGH TIME**

**LOST IN TIME:
THE FOURTH JOURNEY
THROUGH TIME**

DON'T MISS ANY HEROMICE BOOKS!

#1 Mice to the Rescue!

#2 Robot Attack

#3 Flood Mission

#4 The Perilous Plants

#5 The Invisible Thief

#6 Dinosaur Danger

#7 Time Machine Trouble

#8 Charge of the Clones

#9 Insect Invasion

Meet
GERONIMO STILTONOOT

He is a cavemouse—Geronimo Stilton's ancient ancestor! He runs the stone newspaper in the prehistoric village of Old Mouse City. From dealing with dinosaurs to dodging meteorites, his life in the Stone Age is full of adventure!

#1 The Stone of Fire

#2 Watch Your Tail!

#3 Help, I'm in Hot Lava!

#4 The Fast and the Frozen

#5 The Great Mouse Race

#6 Don't Wake the Dinosaur!

#7 I'm a Scaredy-Mouse!

#8 Surfing for Secrets

#9 Get the Scoop, Geronimo!

#10 My Autosaurus Will Win!

#11 Sea Monster Surprise

#12 Paws Off the Pearl!

#13 The Smelly Search

MEET
GERONIMO STILTONIX

He is a spacemouse — the Geronimo Stilton of a parallel universe! He is captain of the spaceship *MouseStar 1*. While flying through the cosmos, he visits distant planets and meets crazy aliens. His adventures are out of this world!

#1 Alien Escape

#2 You're Mine, Captain!

#3 Ice Planet Adventure

#4 The Galactic Goal

#5 Rescue Rebellion

#6 The Underwater Planet

#7 Beware! Space Junk!

#8 Away in a Star Sled

#9 Slurp Monster Showdown